Children's Stories and Poems

Cora Delves

AuthorHouse™
1663 Liberty Drive
Bloomington, IN 47403
www.authorhouse.com
Phone: 1 (800) 839-8640

Published by AuthorHouse   11/27/2018

ISBN: 978-1-5462-6988-5 (sc)
ISBN: 978-1-5462-6989-2 (e)

authorHOUSE®

The Boat Adventure

Another adventure is about to happen because Nana has come for an overnight stay. Each time she comes we lie down on her bed and she has us using our minds for new ideas and quiet time all rolled in one.

This adventure started out as if pretending we were on a large boat. Daddy is the captain and Mommy is the first mate. Daddy takes us out on the boat because the weather is so warm and it is cooler on the water. He drives the boat out into the open water area near an island, it is a strange Island and we are not supposed to go there. At night one can see lights coming from there. Nana shivers as if she is cold.

Peyton and Emelia and Nana are lying on the deck enjoying the warm breeze coming across the bow. They have their swim suits on and getting a tan. Mom and Brother Wyatt are in the cabin resting or playing. Peyton becomes very excited," What is happening" asked Nana? Peyton says that she saw fins in the water, and they are coming nearer. We watch as they come closer and see that a school of Dolphins is having fun playing around our boat. These are not ordinary Dolphins no! They are different because they are all different colors blue and pink, red and brown, lavender and yellow, wow!!

Daddy has anchored the boat so that we can have fun with the Dolphins. Nana asked Daddy to join Emelia and Peyton in the water so that they could see them closer. While the family was in the water splashing each other and laughing, the blue dolphin came closer and then rose on its tail moving backwards and making noises causing everyone to laugh. Then the blue dolphin came close to Nana and indicated that she was to hold onto its fin. Nana took the blue dolphins fin and it swam a few feet away and back again.

Some of the other dolphins joined in by letting Emelia and Peyton and Daddy ride with them. We were having so much fun, being pulled along on the water by the Dolphins and Mom took pictures. Dad suggested that we go diving and see what we would see under the water.

Oh! My! Look Peyton pointed at all the beautiful coral and the different kinds of fish. Such as Rainbow Trout Salmon plus Flatfish and Stingrays and Seahorses, there was Gold fish and so many more. The coral was all colors and sparkled. The ground as a fish or crab skimmed near the bottom of the water moved and shimmered. The seahorses were also very special as they carried mermaids on their backs. Each mermaid had a crown and beautiful color tails. Their names were (Bella, Marianne, Lucille, Elizabeth and Evelina).The mermaid Evelina gave a special crown to Emelia and Peyton. The pink dolphin had swam to the bottom of the water near a coral and found crowns to wear.

We realized that this was a special place. As we explored the bottom of the water Dad and Nana realized that we could breathe like the fish and stay longer in the water. As we swam nearer to the island the dolphins spoke to us and we could understand them. They stated that "they had seen our family in the water before and watched us play. They were really cool dolphins. We held on to their fins again and they had us going around in a big circle, all the other dolphins had joined in and what a fun ride. The sea horses came and gave the girls a ride as well. They were like little aristocrats sitting on them. The male sea horse told us that the males carry the eggs not the female and the girls became very interested to learn more about the species. They saw several pregnant fish and was able to witness as one gave birth .It was amazing to see all those eggs float and be able to bring forth new life. A turtle also told them that they hatch their eggs in the sand on the sea shore. Each year they come back to the same spawning ground. The large Jelly fish was also friendly and didn't stay too close to the little ones. She didn't want to frighten them if they happened to touch her long legs for they could get a shock. It was the jelly fishes way of protecting herself.

Dad and Nana saw how much fun the girls were having and didn't realize that a whale had also come to see and be part of this group. It was a special whale (white)it is called a Beluga whale. Her name was Angel and she belonged to the owners of the Island. Angel had a message for Daddy, she was telling him that a storm was coming and that they should head home. The girls' crowns that were Gold and silver didn't seem like crowns when they came out of the water. It was magic crowns and the air turned them back to coral. The girls kept the crowns in a special place as a memory. Kids all ages love make believe and using their imagination.

It was time to go back into the boat, Mom and Wyatt had lunch ready for them. Peyton and Emelia told Wyatt and Mommy about their adventure. Wyatt wanted to go too. Mom said, "In one more year he could go down to the bottom of the water with the rest of the family" the girls were sad to leave their new friends, but then remembered that they could come again. The crowns would always be theirs and the memories stored in their minds.

As they were eating lunch the weather started to get cooler and the water choppy. Dad decided that it was time to go home. Emelia and Peyton were talking to Mommy about their adventure with Nana and

Daddy. Mom saw a dolphin coming near the boat and something in its beak. So they slowed the boat and accepted the paper from the blue dolphin. It was a special invitation.

It Read:

Your family loves adventures and believes in the world of magic. For your next adventure we invite you to come and visit our Island. We know that you will love it here.

Sincerely
King A. Hager

The girls and Mom were very excited to have such an invitation given to them. All kinds of things popped into Emelia and Peyton's minds and Oh! The questions. "When can we go? They asked. Mommy looked to Nana and said "it was up to Nana as she was the one to take them ". Nana Loves taking the kids on trips like this. So she decided that very soon she would come back and take them to the island with the strange lights at night.

Wow! What an adventure for two little girls. Blue Dolphins, whales, sea horses, coral crowns and a chance to visit a magic island someday.

Enjoy this short story, until your next adventure.

Written by
Cora Delves
May 20th 2012

The lay out for this story is
1. Family on a boat
2. The arrival of Dolphins
3. Picture of them having fun swimming with them
4. The bottom of the sea and coral plus different color fish
5. A white Whale
6. Dolphin giving Dad the paper /invitation

A Magic Island

This story came about as I was visiting some of our grandchildren. I went to stay overnight at their home. In the morning as usual the kids wake up first and come to Nana's bed. I sleep on a blown up mattress and we have what is now known an adventure time. This one such story we created.

This is called "A Magic Mountain" our previous adventure was called "The Boat Ride".

After our adventure on the boat we went to an island. It was not an ordinary island, but a magical island. The sun shining down beautifully and the birds were in the air. There wasn't a cloud in the sky. The sand warm and very inviting for us to" come and explore"

As we walked along the beach Emelia saw the Banana Trees, Peyton saw coconut trees and Wyatt spied the palm trees. They turned to Nana with excitement in their eyes. This is going to be another fun adventure.

There was a gentle breeze blowing and magic could be felt in the air. Along the path they walked, they saw beautiful flowers (small ones, tall and big ones).They came in all shapes and sizes. Nana said" God has given us the rainbow in the color of the flowers".

We kept on exploring and came across a waterfall. With its water cascading over the edge, and pooled in a pond at the bottom while a rainbow covering the pond. Wow! It looked so amazing.

A monkey appeared from behind a tree and he said: "Hi my name is" Ralph" I'm your tour guide while you explore the Island. Wow! A talking monkey? How cool. We were all thirsty by now and Ralph produced glasses as if from thin air. He suggested that we have a drink from the pool. 'Name a color' he said as we each stooped to fill our glasses with water.

Emelia choose orange and her drink looked and tasted like oranges .Peyton chooses purple her favorite color and her drink tasted like grapes. Wyatt likes blue so his choice was blue and everything in his glass tasted like blueberries. Nana had chosen green and her drink tasted like lime-sherbet. Hmm. Gush! This was such fun because the water looked clear as you looked into it.

Ralph then lead us to explore more of the island and suggested that we keep our eyes on the lookout for a castle on the island. As we walked along another pathway the flowers looked like an artist had painted them just for our enjoyment. Their beauty was so overwhelming. Bursts of yellow and orange, lilac and violet, blues red and so many more

Ralph was always smiling (like a monkey smiles) and happy as he lead us to an opening were there was four hammocks. The little ones were tired and had a short nap. As we lay down music soft and low floated on the warm breeze. Music notes floated in the air on a gentle breeze. We wanted to know where it was coming from. Ralph reminded us it was a magic Island and anything could happen. Ralph said" the music came from the trees and sand and the flowers and the birds and the water". The melodious song blending with all the exotic birds on the island soon had us all asleep. Ralph stood watch over us as we napped. After we woke from our nap we started to explore more of the island. The two youngest kids spied the tops of the castle towers first. Oh! The squeals and the jumping. Ralph told us it was very beautiful and sparkly. The castle sparkled due to the Gold Silver with specks of different colors all around the Castle. It took our breath away as we came out into the clearing and our eyes saw it for the first time. The castle had a mote around it and it appeared to sparkle as if diamonds were in the water.

The castle was owned by a royal family whose name was Hager. The King was Abraham Hager, the Queen was Sarah Hager, the Prince was called Dwayne, and the two Princesses were called Jayne and Faye Hager. Their clothes was such beautiful colors (King Hager wore Royal Purple w/Yellow; Queen Hager wore Forest green w/Red; Prince Dwayne wore Royal Blue w/Yellow; Princess Jayne wore Pink and Princess Faye wore Lavender. The young nobles had flowers in their hair and had a silk flower the same color on their dresses. They showed Nana how to make the flowers so Emelia and Peyton could make one to match their dresses at home. The flower layered with a glitter stone in the center then was pinned to their dresses looking Beautiful.

The king suggested to Ralph that he take a break while the royal family showed their visitors more of the castle. The King and Queen took Nana to the Kings special room where there was the family history and they had a cup of tea while they talked. Prince Dwayne took Wyatt to the nursery and he had a nap as he was only two yrs old. Later after he woke up he was given the royal treatment of having a horse ride with Prince Dwayne holding him in his arms .The girls went with the Princess Jayne and Princess Faye to the play room. But not an ordinary playroom no sir it was one with live animals. There they saw and played with some different kinds of animals then had a tea party. Then they too had a short nap. Exploring can be very tiring.

There was a very beautiful stairway with pictures hanging on the walls in all shapes and sizes and they too were not ordinary but magic ones. The objects in the pictures moved as you passed them. Everyone went up and down the stairs several times, because it was fun to watch the objects move. The nobles loved to have fun as well because when it came time to walk back down the stairs the nobles did not walk. They would slide down the bannister. Everyone laughed and had such fun.

Next, we went and saw the towers and dungeons where items were stored for future exploring. We were served a beautiful meal from the fruit trees and gardens outside. They grew their own fruits and vegetables and berries. Then it was to the stables for more adventures. The King and Queen stayed behind and Ralph was with us again. The Prince and Princesses was as excited to go as we were. There we received a big surprise, for Ralph told us that there was not any ordinary horse in there but unusual ones and we learned it was because of their colors. Why there were yellow ones blue ones, pink and lavender ones even a green one. The joy seen on the kids' faces was priceless.

Ralph said "that we were to ride the horses and explore more of the island. Prince Dwayne held Wyatt on the Blue horse, Emelia rode with Princess Jayne on the Pink horse and Peyton rode with Princess Faye on the Lavender horse(that changed its color as they rode).Nana rode the Green horse and Ralph rode the Yellow horse beside Nana. Gush! What a time we are having exclaimed Peyton. Smiling from ear to ear and holding onto the reins. There were so many hills and valleys to explore, from forests 'deep greens and the blues of the ocean below as seen from the hilltops.

As Ralph and Nana rode side by side Ralph confided that "He" was really a magic monkey and the King and Queen had chosen the Delves family to be shown their island as they liked to have adventures. As dusk was coming Nana stated it was time to say Thank You and go home. Maybe we could come again and explore more of the island. There are still lots they haven't seen or explored.

We must have fallen asleep as Nana was telling us this story, because we heard Mommy's voice saying it was time for breakfast before Emelia went to school.

Nana looked at us all and just smiled.

As told to our Grand kids on May 16th, 2012
Written by
Cora Delves
May 22, 2012

Note: In this story, I would like to have pictures of a castle, hammocks with music notes floating in the air and horses in different colors.

The Mountain (story)

"Deep in the rain forest there is a large mountain. Many people believe that anyone can go there and climb this mountain."

Nana had a holiday coming up so what better way to spend it then take her Grandkids on a long trip.

First the kids Emelia Peyton Wyatt and Julia needed backpacks hiking boots and sunglasses and proper clothes suntan lotion first aid kit and compass maps and binoculars .They all had to have an injection shot against infections and bug bites. There is a lot that one must have for such a trip and most important "an imagination".

It took only a day for everyone to be ready and OH! The excitement Emelia stated "that she had paper and pencils to record the journey". Excellent! Says Nana. We'll start out by getting on a train that will take us across Canada and into Africa to the rain forest. As they travelled along they will see such beautiful country and flat land as far as the eye could see. There will be the Rocky Mountains and unending bodies of water as far the eye can see as they travel. In Africa there will be the rain forest and stretches of land were wild animals live and graze. They hope to see some of them and get a picture from a safe distance.

They brought some snacks with them but the main meal of the day was provided by the train porters. Everyone on the train was going to the mystery mountain. There were signs on the train advertising its location and some of the mysteries one could find there. As Nana and the grandkids travelled along on the train, they meet another family named "the Elliotts" sitting in the booth next to them. They had 2 boys and 2 girls a couple of years older than Emelia and Peyton. The kids made friends and time passed quickly.

The Elliotts family names are (John (Dad) Mary (mother) sons Mark and Lucas and their daughters Sally and Ashley) John and Mary asked" if they could join our family for the climb up the mountain?" Why not! This is an adventure which all the kids will enjoy stated "Nana".

As they crossed Canada they saw the mountains with white snow top peaks. In areas it looked like the snow was drifting and caused a mist on top of the mountains. Further down could be seen as if an avalanche was happening. The rolling of the snow as it came down the side of the mountain was magnificent to watch. Everyone agreed on that point, but, they also agreed that they were glad to be safe on the train.

The prairies were so vast that they saw for miles only sparse trees or bushes. Farmers had their land all cropped and some were still planting or harvesting in the fields. It will be something to remember the rest of their young lives. As they cross the border into Africa it became apparent that the green grass and long vegetation was different than anything they had ever seen. For not only was the land different the animals was too.

There were elephants on the edge of the trees and giraffes slowing walking around. There was a large water pond and animals stopped to have a drink. Some even went into it had a dip. The train slowed down some so folks could enjoy the scenery and what the animals were doing. Time to take a few pictures and have a laugh or two about the antics the animals were doing. Then before they knew it they had reached their destination. Then as the train stops everyone prepares to get off the train.

Once they step outside everyone can see the mountain of in the distance. The area around them is strange and the buildings are small and made of orange stones. You feel the relaxation and excitement in the air. Everyone is ready to start walking the pathway towards the mountain. The sun is hidden behind some clouds and everyone hopes it doesn't turn to rain. But good travelers are prepared for anything.

Of in the far distance everyone could see water cascading over the side of the mountain and it has a shimmer to it. Julia and Sally looked at each other and giggled.' Hey is that water colored"? Asked Sally and Julia at the same time and they giggled some more. Then they moved their little bodies to mimic the water.

As they walk along the older boys Mark and Lucas took Wyatt with them and he looks so grown up. Wyatt is chattering like a magpie asking "Why is that tree all orange? How come the paths are the color purple?" Mark and Lucas turn to their sisters and suggest they play a game called" I Spy". The idea was to see who could find a new object as they walked along the path. There was orange trees, grape bushes, pink rabbits, yellow snakes multi colored rocks and oh my all the different kinds of trees. Emelia was so busy enjoying her trip she forgot to take notes, but that's ok too. John, Mary and Nana joined in as well and before they knew it the mountain loomed before them. Wow!! Now they understood why so many people wanted to climb this mountain.

The sun came out from behind the clouds and a wonderful sight was seen. This mountain wasn't green or brown but all the colors of oranges one can imagine. The five girls took pictures starting at the bottom of the mountain all the way to the top. There was a sign that read "Have one treat from the tree and please don't be greedy or you won't reach the top of the mountain" What a strange sign! All the girls exclaimed.

Nana was just behind the group and very quiet and thinking and Emelia felt that might be a bad sign. She asked" Nana what's wrong?" Nana looked at her and smiled." Oh! I was just thinking if anyone really did make it to the top of the mountain". For as far as the eye could see there were all types of fruit trees and berry bushes even trees with candy on them (wrapped of course).

Peyton looked at Emelia and Julia and said "I have an Idea. Maybe we should walk to the top of the mountain and on the way down have a treat from the trees". This made sense to Nana, Mary and John. The other kids told her she was "silly". "We'll see" she answered. So they started to walk up the mountain. The older kids every once in a while would eat a treat from one tree or another on their way up the mountain. Their pockets overflowing with wrapped candy and fresh fruit.

The trees on the bottom of the mountain held gum drops and cherries, bananas, s'more bars, gummy bears, candy canes, bubble gum, apples, oranges, hard wrapped candy and soft wrapped candy.

Some trees were laden with pears and plums as well. Peyton Julia and Wyatt would smell the sweets but kept on walking up the path. Soon they were half way up the mountain and the older boys were complaining about a stomach ache Emelia had eaten as well but not enough to make her feel ill.

Everyone stopped at the inlet provided for emergencies; there were benches for folks to seat on or lie down if need be. Emelia and Peyton removed their backpacks and took out the first aid kits. Nana and Emelia looked after the girls and Peyton and Mary and John looked after the boys. The older boys and girls received" Pepto Bismo tablets" to settle their stomachs. Young Lucas was worst then the others so Peyton asked "his parents what she could give him". The Elliotts thanked the girls for being so well prepared and smart with their first aid. The Elliotts were not prepared because they hadn't known what to expect to see on the trip. They just thought it was an ordinary mountain and hiking was always a fun family thing.

The group rested for a short time and let the medicine work on the kids' stomach. No one was going to be left behind or the group to be separated for any reason. The friendship was important to the kids and they were having a good time despite the setback.

Everyone started off again and before you knew it they had reached the top of the mountain. At the top they meet a lady named "Angie".

She had long blonde hair and blue eyes and a long flowing pink dress with long sleeves that covered her finger tips. It was her job to check everyone and make sure that they were ok and no one else was sick. It was also Angles job to answer any questions that the families might have about the Mountain. The oldest boys looked like they were going to throw up so Angie gave them some more medicine. She asked" if they had read the sign at the beginning of the path before starting their journey." Wyatt so innocent stated no! Angie asked' why not?" Wyatt answered "I cannot read everything. Everyone smiled and laughed even Wyatt. It is always important to read the signs and try and follow the instructions. It is for your own health and wellbeing.

Angie asked everyone "what other things they had seen on their way up the mountain?" Peyton stated "that she had seen a yellow moose and Wyatt a ruby rabbit". Sally stated "that she saw different kinds of birds in the trees and was amazed at how quiet they were. Don't they sing she asked? Yes! Angie replied 'one must stop along the way and really listen to their song". Ashley said 'that she noticed all the different colors in the forest. There are so many different shades of orange and it is beautiful."

Angie asked the adults "What they saw and how they felt about the mountain". The Elliotts said" that they didn't see any color except the shades of green and browns". Nana smiled because she knew that some adults have no make believe in them. Your mind is a beautiful thing, let it explore and open to all you see. Nana suggested to John and Mary that" they pretend to see things differently from that moment forward" to take a second look at things around them and see if it's still green and brown.

John and Mary walked over to the lookout post and observed what was around them. Then turning toward each other they smiled and for the first time could see what everyone else saw. All the magic on the Mountain, the color orange, the birds and animals and oh such a wonderful water fall sound as it tumbled off the side of the mountain. This was no ordinary waterfall for it did shimmer as it was cascading over the mountain. In the water lived silver fish and silver grass which gave the illusion of the shimmer. Everyone spent time wondering back and forth across the platform and enjoying the different views. Every time some person saw something different they would let the others know and they would move to that spot so they could see it as well. The group spent a couple of hours on the Mountain top and enjoyed all the beauty surrounding them. Asking Angie many questions and the laughter and giggles could be heard from lower down the mountain.

It was time to go back down the mountain. As they started back down; the path they had to take a different one to see more of the wonders and they came across another sign, "you may have a treat from what you see. Enjoy and don't forget to share" Another strange sign the boys said as a chorus and smiled. Emelia and Peyton smiled at one another and held their secret. They knew what it meant. Yes, they did take treats (only one) from the different kinds of trees and bushes. (Apples and oranges and candy canes and chocolate and bubble gum) Instead of eating one piece of fruit or candy every time, they put some of them in their backpacks to share when they got on the train or at home.

Coming down the mountain they saw and heard more. The birds were singing so they stopped and listened. Many of the animals with different colors would change color according to their surroundings or as they came out of their hiding places amongst the trees. The animals would walk up to the families and allowed the folks to pet them. Then as the families got closer to the bottom of the mountain they met Angie again. She smiled and asked "How they enjoyed their journey?"

They all agreed it was a great time. The two families had made friends. They had great fun walking up and down the mountain and watch as the colors changed in the trees. "They learned that you don't always have to have what you see. Sharing is much more fun" Peyton and Emelia dug into their backpacks and gave Angie some of the special treats they had collected. Angie smiled and placed her hand on top of theirs and said "Thank You", but when she took her hands away both of the girls received a big surprise. For in their hands was a replica of the mountain to keep as a treasure. The girls hugged Angie and said "Thank You". Yes, Angie is magical too.

Nana smiled at everyone all around her. Even Nana loves a good surprise. The train trip home was quiet for everyone was tired. Nana wrote down what Emelia had not for she knew Emelia needed her rest and enjoyed the adventure as well. John and Mary also made notes about what they saw and how happy the children looked and sounded. It is one trip they'll treasure forever.

As the story ends Nana looks at the two youngest children Julia and Wyatt and is surprised to find them fast asleep on the rug.

Written By
Cora Delves
May 20, 2012

The Sandwich

Kids of all ages love making and eating sandwiches. Why there is egg sandwiches, cheese, tuna, bologna, banana, nutella, peanut butter and jelly the list is endless.

Because kids love sandwiches I thought it would be a good topic to talk about. Now I'm not so sure.

Peyton and Wyatt and Julia were playing outside for a few hours. Between paying ball, hopscotch and swings, pretending they were fishing using the jumping ropes tied to a stick as fishing poles and a smaller stick for a hook it was a busy morning for them and the sun was making them sweaty and thirsty.it was also near lunch time and their tummy told them to eat. They turned to their Mom and asked her for some food.

What would you like to eat for lunch? Mac & Cheese? Or a Fruit plate, soup, hotdogs? Well! Wyatt said "popcorn". Popcorn? That's not enough you'll still be hungry from all you're playing outside. Peyton volunteered to make sandwiches. I can do it all by myself. As if that said it all Mom smiled.

So Mom went to the fridge and took out the bread, Wyatt went to the cupboard and pointed to the peanut butter Julia asked for

Nutella. (Some of the kids pronounce it tunella). Peyton stood on her chair washed her hands and Mom stood behind her for safety. Mom let Peyton spread on the peanut butter and watched as Peyton stuck out her tongue as she busily made sandwiches for Wyatt, Julia and herself. Then Peyton turned to her Mom and asked would you like one too Mom? I'll make it for you.

So with two more pieces of bread Peyton makes Mom a sandwich. Priceless are the kids as they try and do as grown- ups do. They may have accidents while making them like dropping the jam on the counter or lick their fingers because the honey has run down their fingers. It is fun to watch as kids make sandwiches.

Then after all is done Mom gets to clean the kitchen up. Yes the kids got their popcorn too.

Written by
Cora Delves
May 25th, 2012

Gingerbread Man-1

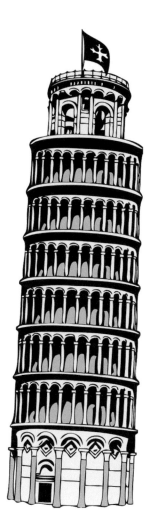

The name alone gives you the idea that it is a cookie. Well! Guess what it is not. This gingerbread man is real (in the make believe world anyway).This is a short story about how a person who was from the warmer climates and because his skin color was different they called him gingerbread man.

A fellow loved to travel and meet people. He could play any kind of musical instrument wind or string. The children loved to hear and watch him preform. They would learn lot of things about the world we live in through the Gingermans travels.

The Leaning Tower of Pizza was a very tall building and he made the kids laugh when described it as a pizza (like the kind you eat). He had put mushrooms, pepperonis, ham, pineapples beacon, cheese and peppers tomatoes, and all kinds of food on the tower.

The children were very involved in this story because the Gingerbread Man got them to pretend that they were making the "Leaning Tower of Pizza" too. The kids were up and down twisting, turning laughing, and enjoying themselves.

By the end of the Gingerbread Mans' story, the adults realized that the kids had put in 45 minutes of physical activity. The kids were now hungry and thirsty. Can you guess what they had to eat? Yes! That is right they had pizza with all the different kind of toppings mentioned in the story.

Cora Delves
November 11th, 2012

The Gingerbread Man-2 Visits to the Jungle

The gingerbread man went to the jungle for he had heard so many different things about it.

He took the plane to a place called Africa. Although there is many places well inhabited there is still a jungle too. He went to visit the jungle with a tour group carrying their backpack and bedrolls and tents. The day was sunny and warm when they started on their journey but very exciting. Finding what different animals and vegetation, and tall trees in the forest

Early morning brought the insects around them and people became upset that the Gingerbread man was not. They asked him his secret. Well he answered it depends on what you eat and how you dress that makes the difference. In addition, I used protection on my skin.

He smiled at them and started asking questions of his own. How many of you have seen the tiger that was 15 yards off to the North a short while ago? On the other hand, the snake that was beside Mr. Thompson as we took a water break.

Everyone looked around and became more attentive as they walked through the jungle. The tour group asked more questions of the guide and soon all became so involved in their surroundings that the insects and bites forgotten.

They found a clearing in the middle of nowhere and decided to set up their tents for the night. Each took turns gathering wood for a fire and making a meal over the open flames. Some of the folks in the group had never camped before and found it to be an excellent adventure.

The tour guide asked the group as they settled for the evening if someone was good telling stories or leading in camp songs. One young chap brought forth his harmonica and they had a good sing along. Then the Gingerbread man asked the young man to play softly as he told a story about a bear lost in a coalmine.

Everything grew quiet as he spoke. He stood and walked around the group as he talked. The folks were so interested in Him that they did not see a leopard wonder into their camp sight. Gingerbread man slowly walked over to the guide while keeping the others entertained and whispered in his ear about the leopard.

As any good guide should, he carried a gun with him. In addition, a blow dart that would stun any animal if a group was there and did not want to cause a panic.

Very slowly, he withdrew the blowgun and used it on the leopard. The animal fell down beside the young chap playing the harmonica. Some folks jumped up and ran into their tents while others remained and looked the leopard over. The strongest of the men carried the leopard away from the campsite. Hurting him was not the intention.

After things had settled down from the excitement of the unexpected visitor, everyone gave the Gingerbread Man an applause for his smart thinking and the way he alerted their guide. Taking turns at the campfire and watching for more wonders the folks slept throughout the night.

Early morning breakfast was eaten tents packed away and then they headed back to the hotel where everyone stayed. Somehow, the news about the leopard was already known at the hotel and many other people came to hear about the adventure.

The tour guide explained what had happened and that all was safe. Due to The Gingerbread Mans, quick thinking and calm approach to the guide all were safe.

The gingerbread Man had enjoyed his trip and made many new friends.

Written by
Cora Delves
Sept.23, 2018

The Circus

The Circus is coming to town. Everyone was getting excited because that meant school was almost over and hot summer days ahead. There would be day trips to the beach and family cottages to hang at, friends staying overnight and camp outs in the back yard. Yahoo.

This year the circus was going to be a little different. We are all looking forward to the high wire acts, the animal acts, the clowns and their magic shows plus the puppy dog show is always a crowd pleaser.

The board walk is always interesting as well. There are so many different types of games to play and different venders selling their wares. There is even people whom give away free items or next to cost. They have competitions for people to enter and try and win the big prize. The cooking shows are great too, you sit and watch as the chef cooks and explains how such a product is so great to use. They hand out samples of what he is cooking and sometimes there is a sample on a smaller scale of the instruments he is using given free to people whom answer the question correctly and fast.

The day the circus comes we watch as they parade through town. The high wire performers hand out flyers inviting everyone to come to the circus and see the new additions. The band plays and some of the animals walk along beside their trainers while doing a trick or two. The kids and adults smile and you can feel the excitement in the air.

The monkeys riding on the clowns shoulders would makes faces at the crowds on the sidewalks and kids were heard asking their parents "when can we go to see the circus"?

School is over so the next day Nana and Papa took Emelia and Peyton while Mommy and Daddy took Wyatt and Katherine and William took Julia to see the circus. The kids haven't been to a circus before so going as a family was a good way to go.

Nana and Papa took the girls to the kids' games and there they had so much fun trying to win a prize. The one game they played was called the duck pond. Each duck had a size of the prize written on the bottom of the duck, so first you had catch the duck and then the vender would turn it over and show you what you won. Papa only won a key chain; Emelia won a medium size whale. Julia won a medium size dog and Peyton won a large teddy bear, it was bigger than her. (Guess who got to carry it around all day, yep it was Papa).

Next we went to the petting zoo area. There we saw all kinds of small animals like rabbits, lambs, foals and calves, then there was puppy dogs; cat with her kittens, gerbils, white mice, (Nana hates mice she shivers and steps back). There were goats, llamas, Shetland ponies, deer, pigs, chicken and chicks, roasters and many more small animals.

We meet the rest of the family while there and Wyatt loved the animals as well. You could hear him say "Look Dad, Look Mom. Come see Julia and Peyton. We bought food to feed the animals as they were only allowed with some of the foods they were fed at home with. There was an animal keeper there watching to see how much was given to the animals and that no animal was hurt or push around. It was very organized.

As we made our way to the go carts for some fun on the track one could hear music played very loud, people shouting " get your ticket here".(roarrrr, roarrrr) one lap around the track took 15 minutes and each person was allowed 3 turns. As we drove around the track one could see three big tents on the other side of the fair grounds. One held the high wire acts, another the animal acts and the third was with clowns because they had a cannon act. So many tents because it was safer to keep things in one area instead of having to always move them for the next act. What a variety to see or do at the circus. One could probably return several days and still not see everything.

As one came to the top of the race track you could see the three old fashion airplanes that was the main attraction at the circus this year. They were not planes to just look at; the flyer stated that people could take a ride in them. This was special because as long as a child was with an adult they could go for a ride in the plane. So after we finished on the go cars guess who went on the planes. Yes, that's right Nana Papa; Emelia and Peyton bought tickets and went up. The attendant came and gave them life jackets to put on so they wouldn't be cold. She looked at the kids and asked "are you ready for some fun"? Yes Mam! We sure are the girls replied.

So they were on their way, everyone buckle up she said and keep all limbs inside the plane, helmets came next, they felt a difference in the plane it was moving. Don't be afraid Emelia, Nana said as she instructed her to look down and watch as the people became smaller like ants and the houses like boxes. Now look at the mountain why it isn't so big now. The pilot took us over the fairgrounds and we saw our family waiting below for their turn. They're going to freak said Peyton. Papa laughed and thought to himself, I'm doing that now and you don't know it kido.

The pilot points to her left and we turned and saw a beautiful waterfall on one side of the mountain. Wow! This came from Emelia as she saw a big rainbow fill the air above the flowing water below. One could feel as if you were able to go sliding along the rainbow. It sure is nice up here I never knew that was there stated Papa as he lived in this town all his life.

The girls were able to see the sky above and around them also what was below due to some kind and thoughtful people whom had placed a glass floor in the plane so you could enjoy the ride. The children were so excited and couldn't wait to talk to Mom and Dad and see how they liked the ride.

It was also Julia's first ride and she went with her Mom and Dad. The four kids came away from the plane rides higher than a kite. Did you see us go zoom asked Wyatt as he pretends he is a plane. Julia asked if anyone saw all the clouds (what clouds?) William had told her that the smoke from the other planes was clouds so she wouldn't believe the plane was on fire.

It was getting close to supper time so everyone walked back to the cars and talked for a short while about the fun at the circus before going home to a good meal, warm bath and bed. Bed time for everyone that night was early.

We knew it was going to be the best circus for them ever.

Written by
Cora Delves
May 25th, 2012

Fishing

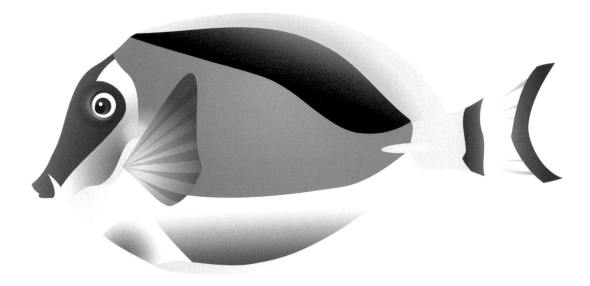

Adam has been teaching his daughters how to fish at an early age. They started by practicing holding a fishing rod. Next Dad added a plastic fish to Emelia's line and taught her how to cast. They did this for weeks because Emelia wanted the real thing not just watch her Dad. Therefore, Adam decided to add fish bait to the rod and show Emelia how to cast.

Any good angler knows that casting takes time to learn and using a plastic fish is disappointing. Having to stay closer to the shore is horrible. Emelia would walk closer to the end of the deck and drop her line in the water. Emelia would call her Daddy and say, "I did it"

Papa always stood near Emelia to make sure she did not fall into the water. Papa would bring along his fishing rod as well. Together they had fun and soon Emelia would try harder to practice casting her line. She was enjoying it more and more. This is only another step or part of fishing. Daddy also will teach her how to untangle a fish so she will not get hurt. For several weeks, they went outside on the docks and practiced. Emelia was very patient although she never caught anything. Then one Saturday morning Emelia caught more than her Dad did. She was so excited.

After a few weeks, the girls Emelia and Peyton became better at fishing. There were times Emelia caught more fish than her Father did. They wanted to go on a fishing trip. Dad looked on the internet for a favorite fishing ground. In the area, there was a fishing derby for families coming up.

They called the North Bay conservation and learned that a fishing derby was to take place the coming weekend. Dad asked if there was room for another family. Sure, this weekend is a derby for beginners, youth and seniors. It was trout season and only adults needed a fishing license. Dad and the girls left the house for a few hours and when they came home, they had not only a license for Dad but also a cooler to keep the fish in plus hooks and bait and other cool stuff. Chairs to sit on, water bottles and a bucket to put fish into until weighed and measured. The girls hoped they would catch the heaviest or longest fish.

The day had arrived for Emelia to do her first real fishing. Adam and Emelia got up early and went into the back yard to collect worms. They put them in a container to keep them fresh. Emelia asked her Dad, "Why worms? Well, Dad said, "fish love fresh worms "they wiggle on the hook and it gets the fish's attention.

On the day of the derby all went even Papa and Nana. Wow! there are so many people here exclaimed Emelia. Yes said Mom and after you and Daddy register and get a number we will find our spot.

Children under seven did not need a license and received a new fishing rod, bait and a hat plus a guidebook and sunglasses. It was fantastic! The weather was hot and a gentle breeze was blowing in off the water. There were food vendors and clowns, face painting and more.

The folks at the derby gave the kids time to find a spot and they had to carry a bucket with water in it for the fish to stay alive. After the fish was weighted, it was then set free. The category was determined by the children's ages. The girls were catching more fish than their Dad was. Peyton had help from Papa and Nana. They looked at their

Dad and realized he was upset, because his line had become tangled on the bottom of the water. Adam tried to unhook it but to no avail. Emelia had been watching her Dad and did not realize that a big fish was caught on her line. Adam had decided to cut the line when he noticed that his knife was not in his belt loop. He tried to reach for his tackle box when he heard a splash. He glanced at the girls but Emelia was not there. Peyton started to cry because a fish had pulled her big sister into the water. Adam dropped his fishing rod and called to those in hearing to watch Peyton as he jumped into the water after Emelia. Emelia had not let go in time to save herself. Emelia swam to the top of the water were her Dad was looking for her.

The fish that had pulled Emelia into the water also rose to the top and he said (guess what? you did not put on your life jacket) Dad and Emelia were in shock (did you hear that fish talk they asked each other?) Folks near helped them out of the water. The lifeguard on duty /first aid person on duty checked Emelia out to make sure she was ok. Dad gave Emelia and Peyton a big hug. The girls were scared for a short time but did not want to stop fishing. They did not win any trophies for fishing, but received one for the excitement of the day and their strength to keep going and have fun.

The winners received a new bike plus a season pass for fishing. The pass was for the adults, as the child had to be accompanying with a parent. Each child left the derby feeling happy and excited. Spending the day with their parents, catching fish and receiving a new fishing rod was the highlight of the day. Some kids were heard to say," When is the next fishing derby?"

Sunburns ignored and spending hours in the open air was the best adventure ever.

Written by
Cora Delves
May22, 2012

`Note in this story;
  1. Fishing with parents
  2. Plastic fish on a rod
  3. Emelia and Dad in the water with a fish near them
  4. All folks smiling and having a good day

Thunder Storms

The clashing and roaring of the storm outside
The thunder makes the earth quake
The boards in the house moan
The family lies in their beds waiting and wondering
Will this ever stop?

The sky lights up with strikes of lighting
It is like a show put on by the Angels
It is one of Gods wonders of art.
One can watch each strike of lighting
While staying in a safe place to observe
This marvelous sight

The house is quiet all sleeping in their cozy beds
Outside the storm is starting to slow down.
The roaring sound of thunder is miles away
No longer heard rolling overhead

The gentle sound of rain
Hitting the window pane
Lulls one to sleep for a good rest
The storm is over.

Written by:
Cora Delves
Oct.03, 2016

Winter's Breathe

It is that time of year when, one needs to bundle up warm
To avoid the cold breathe of winter
There are people who will embrace the breathe of winter
When they go skiing and hiking or winter ice fishing

The day shines bright and fair as the sun shines down upon us
The trees stir in the air due to the breathe of winter
So no matter how one embraces the winter season
We cannot appreciate it without the cool breathe of winter

Written by
Cora delves
Jan.16th 2012

Note: I am not a poet but there are at times when I need to write down
what I am feeling.

The Tree

I'm a lovely tree, my branches grow strong and free

They reach up to the sky as they seem to say "Look at Me"

For years I grew stronger and stronger

I stood against the Rain, Sun and Wind

Then came one icy winter's day

The elements were so strong they wore me down

So that my branches spread apart and like a mushroom I felt

My branches so spread apart that some even bowed on the ground.

I lay prostrate before my Lord the maker

I felt beaten and was reminded that

Although I was a strong and beautiful tree

For all to see and admire, I was made by God

Who brought me back to life

Written by

Cora Delves

March 14th 2014

This poem is written about a true winters, storm. The tree is real and beautiful and that winter I saw as it was spread wide open through the middle. I never thought it would survive the winter but it did and has grown to its healthy self. I have a picture of it before the storm.

It is found in Cope town, Ontario.

Based on a true event. There was a winter storm and then in the spring this tree survived.

Winter is over

Winters over and my limbs
are growing strong
The sunshine gives me heat
as I slowly come along
The children gather round
to see my buds
As they begin to bloom

The winter storms are leaving
The buds are breaking
through the earth
The birds in the air merrily chirping
Letting everyone know that spring is here.

Soon all Gods' creatures will see
That summer is here and they'll rejoice
My strength will be fully restored
But, I'll always remember the lesson
From winters Icy Storm.

Written by
Cora Delves
April 9th 2014

The Stallion

Out on the open field galloping
He races along so magnificently
His coat black as coal
Glistening from the sweat

Galloping to a tune only he knows
Others have tried to race him
But alas they cannot
For he is a lone Stallion

He stands about 20 hands high
His length is anyone's guess
The marking on his forehead
Looks like a star.

He can be seen many a time
Standing still watching
He will hear people
Talking but not come forth

For soon he will be galloping
Once again across the field
Racing against the wind
To the tune in his head.

WRITTEN By
Cora Delves
March 23, 2017

The First Stars of Spring

We gaze up into the sky; it is filled with the stars on high
They shine brightly from above, giving us all their love.
They twinkle and sparkle like little jewels
Found in a necklace on the ground.

The heavens are alive with them and you can
feel the energy and joy they give
Walking along under their brightness
holding your hand and whispering
It feels like a heavenly body has entered our world
So we carefully observe the stars in their
entire splendor and make a wish.

Tomorrow will be another day: but tonight belongs to us
We enjoy each moment we spend in the moonlight and the stars.
It calms us and showers us with its peace.

Written by
Cora Delves
March 22, 2017

Swans

Today I saw a swan as it appeared out of the sky so snowy white.
The swan hides in the clouds while in flight.
The other birds gather around him
Following him slowly as they land and walk about
The Swam is a sure sign that summer is around the corner
Then the winter's cold winds will be over.

Written by
Cora Delves
Feb.21,2017

Wind

To hear the wind outside it makes one think

There is a storm swirling about.

I looked outside and could see nothing.

There was brightness to the sky

For such a late hour

It sounds at time like a train is passing close to the house

As if it might come through and knock everything down

Then after a few minutes it gets quiet

So you figure it's gone

But no! There it is again

The roaring swishing sounds of the wind

Racing through the trees

At times one can imagine the feel of the breeze

As it passes by the home

Maybe it will soothe the soul and let one rest.
Yes the sounds of the swishing winds
All around us can be heard

Written by
Cora Delves
Feb.12, 2017

Together

We sit on the balcony and what do we see
Buildings, parks all aglow from the morning sun
It reflects of the windows and vehicles as they pass by
The colors in the world appear brighter by far

The warmth flowing into us as we sit and relax
The splendor of the park and the wondrous sounds
It feels surreal and tranquil we sip our drinks and smile
We enjoyed the view relaxing on the balcony

The mountains rise above the city and its splendor
Shows the world that it is beautiful
The winter greens and blossoms flowing along its pathways
People exploring the treasures hidden within

The sun shining on the forest makes it appear
as if magic can be found within
The birds singing, animals wondering under
bushes and making a home
The water falls hidden for people to enjoy at journey's end
They swim and fish and relax in its warmth

Yes as we sit on the balcony relaxing

We enjoy the mountains, people scurrying along the roads

Enjoying each other's thoughts and company

Life goes on as we sit here on the balcony.

Written by

Cora Delves

Feb.5th 2017

Hugs

Hugs are a very precious thing
They come in all shapes and forms
It isn't just one person holding another
It's the warmth that is given to another

Giving a child a new toy for no special reason
Helping a stranger with directions
Giving food and clothing to the unfortunate

A friend is having a bad day
So kind words go a long way
So hugs mean different things
To all kinds of people

Share your warmth and hugs
To family; Friends; Animals and Strangers
God well repay in kind
When you too need a hug.

Written by
Cora Delves
Feb.7th 2017

My Hug for You

The sun is shining from above
Is the warmth I give to you.
The gentle breeze surrounding you is my arms
Together they comfort you.
My Hug for you.

Written by
Cora Delves
Feb.7th 2017

Coco

My friend Coco is a dog
She loves to cuddle all day long.
I tried to walk her, and
she climbs on my feet
Coco nips at my toes and
jumps in her sleep
With blonde fur and a dark snout
She sure it cute to have about.
So my friend I'll feed and watch her grow
Then someday along the road we'll go
I hold her leash while she holds a bone.

Written by
Cora Delves
Nov 29th 2016

Eyes

The eyes are our windows
They let us see the blue sky
Green grass meadows, mountains
The glow on people's faces
The happening's surrounding us.
The most beautiful colors in the world
The fashions of the past and future
So treasure your eyes for they are
The windows to our world

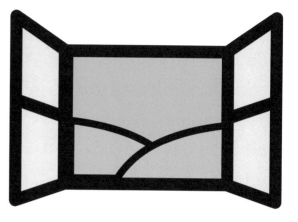

Written by
Cora Delves
June 20, 2014

A Blessing

The sky is glowing
All around us
As on our journey we go
The sun beams bless us
The stars guide us
As we near our goal
Travel far and wide
Remember God is
Always by our side.

Written by
Cora Delves
March 4th, 2010

Life's a Journey

They walk along enjoying themselves

Not a care in the world

The sun shines down as smiles glow

Still onward they go

They walk and talk and laugh

Having a good stroll

The young gathering information

Ask questions, having fun

Still onward they go

There's many an adventure

Both good and bad

Enjoy each step along the path

As onward they go

Written by

Cora delves

June 19th 2014

Children's' Innocence

The children play out on the grass
Jumping rope and toss the ball
Blowing bubbles in the air and then tries to catch them
The weather is warm
Skies have fluffy white clouds
The kids lie on the ground
Watching as they pass overhead
I see a rabbit says one little girl
I see a whale answers the boy
The rest also try and find
Items or shapes in the sky
Music flows through the house
Mothers are doing their housework
The kids are doing their homework
All the kids are having fun
Playing outside in the Sun

Written by
Cora Delves
Sept.17th. 2012

The Clouds

Above the clouds we soar
They are like a fluffy pillow below
They roll along as waves on the shore
We glide over them
Feel as if we're in
The hands of God

As we glance out the window
The sun spreads its Golden Rays
What a beautiful sight
Quiet and serene to look upon
One of Natures' most
Beautiful delights

Written by
Cora Delves
Aug.11th,2012

The Plane

As the plane glides across the sky
It carries passengers from all walks of life
To new adventures and back

Some are going on Holidays
Some going back home
Both young and old relax
Put their trust in the pilots
To get them safely there

They see from the windows the rain
Falling down on the earth
Oh! What a sight to watch as rain falls
From the clouds beside you

Such a wonderful miracle
A memory to hold
In ones' mind forever

Written by
Cora Delves
Aug.8ᵗʰ 2012

The Ground

The ground was brown and bare
When I woke up this morning
The snow was felt in the air

Now as I go to work
The sky opens up and snow
Starts to fly

So now the ground
Is no longer brown and bare
It's now as white
As my Mother's hair.

Written by
Cora Delves
Jan.28, 2017

Snow and Wind Dancing

The Snow and Wind are dancing
Swaying to and fro
First one leads than the other
Swaying to and fro.

As they dance the ground grows whiter
People scurrying to get out
Of the weather
As it sways to and fro.

But not to worry for
It soon will be over
Then there will not be anymore
Snow and Wind dancing
Swaying to and fro.

Written by
Cora Delves
Jan. 28th,2017

Rainy Day Blues

The little girl sat at the window sighed and said
Oh! Why must it rain? For now I cannot go out and play.
Her Mother asked "What's wrong Suzy?"
The little girl replied 'Why it's raining outside."

Don't worry Suzy Mother said" we can play in here.
How? Asked Suzy, I'm stuck in this chair.
Mother smiled and said we'll pretend we are in an
Open glass boat on the ocean.

See there goes a whale wagging its tail
As a big truck passed by the window
Sending sprays of water from the puddle on the ground
Suzy smiled and said I'm going to love playing

In this big glass boat
Then a school of fish went past.
Suzy watched as a load of kids
Getting off the school bus started running through the rain.

Suzy and her Mother spent
Many hours playing in the glass boat
Chasing the rainy day blues away.

Written by
Cora Delves
Jan.28,2017

Snow Flakes falling from Heaven.

The skies open up and from them fall white sparkles
We call them snowflakes
They melt very fast as they reach the ground
To capture a snow flake up close is tricky
One has to wait for just that right moment in time.

To then blow it up and see for real
Just exactly how a snow flake is made
The spirals and twists and pointed edges.
In the cool air they give the reflection of sparkles.

It is caused by the different temperatures in the air
The sun shining down on them reflecting
The prisms and showing us what a
World God has made for us to enjoy.

Written by
Cora Delves
Jan.14th, 2017
Picture was taken by cousin
Michele Griffin

Lily

The lilies in the field grow straight and tall
They look so sweet and beautiful
It is a shame to pluck them

Beautiful flowers were meant to be shared
To loved ones far and near.
The white reminds us of purity
Yellow the golden sun shining above
The fragrance as it drifts in the warm breeze.

God gave us these beautiful flowers
Not only a symbol of his love but,
For us to remember Him as well.
God has created a wondrous world and
It is for us to look after it.

Enjoy the lilies in the field,
Their fragrance, beauty
Close your eyes and inhale.
Yes just close your eyes and inhale.

The lilies in the field grow straight and tall.

Written by
Cora Delves
October 23, 2016

Home

Home is more than buildings were people live
Home is the feeling you get with others
The warm glow of love that surround you as you mingle
The look on the faces that love one another

The inner peace you feel.
One doesn't need riches to show love
It is the gentle sharing of feelings,
The warm hugs and laughter.
Sitting side by side with a cup of coffee
And enjoying a good conversation.

The laughter as you share a good snowball fight
The good news that a new generation is starting
These are a few of what makes a home.
Lying on a rug before the fire
Reading a book or playing scrabble.

Yes there are a lot of different things
That helps to make a home.

Written by
Cora Delves
October 23, 2016

Thunder Storms

The clashing and roaring of the storm outside
The thunder makes the earth quake
The boards in the house moan
The family lies in their beds waiting and wondering
Will this ever stop?

The sky lights up with strikes of lighting
It is like a show put on by the Angels
It is one of Gods wonders of art.
One can watch each strike of lighting
While staying in a safe place to observe
This marvelous sight

The house is quiet all sleeping in their cozy beds
Outside the storm is starting to slow down.
The roaring sound of thunder is miles away
No longer heard rolling overhead

The gentle sound of rain
Hitting the window pane
Lulls one to sleep for a good rest
The storm is over.

Written by:
Cora Delves
Oct.03, 2016

Mountains of Home

Behind our home, the mountains climb
They are magnificent, and look very lush
The green can be seen for miles
The sight is a wonder to behold.

To wake up in the morning after a thunder storm
To hear the birds singing in the trees,
The gentle rustle of the branches,
As they sway in the breeze.

One can pick up the sound of the waterfall
This is seen on one side of the mountain,
As it gently flows over the rocks
It's so peaceful that to walk away hurts

One is tempted to linger on their patio
Have that one more cup of tea, close their eyes and relax.
Listen to the music it creates. The birds singing
Water rippling, branches swaying,
Heaven!

Written by
Cora Delves
Oct.3, 2016

Printed in the United States
By Bookmasters